WILD
ADVENTURES

To Melker and Kristina Granström for happy times
and wild adventures shared in Lapland – *Mick and Brita*

JANETTA OTTER-BARRY BOOKS

Wild Adventures © Frances Lincoln Limited 2015
Text and illustrations © Mick Manning and Brita Granström 2015

First published in Great Britain and in the USA in 2015 by
Frances Lincoln Children's Books,
74-77 White Lion Street,
London N1 9PF
www.franceslincoln.com

A CIP catalogue record for this book is available from the British Library

ISBN 978-1-84780-436-5

The illustrations in this book are in pencil and watercolour.
Mick has done most of the natural history drawings while Brita has drawn the people, a selection of the plants, some seaside creatures and the hand lettering.
Find out more about Mick and Brita's books at: www.mickandbrita.com.

Printed in China

1 3 5 7 9 8 6 4 2

WILD
ADVENTURES

Mick Manning & Brita Granström

F

FRANCES LINCOLN
CHILDREN'S BOOKS

Contents

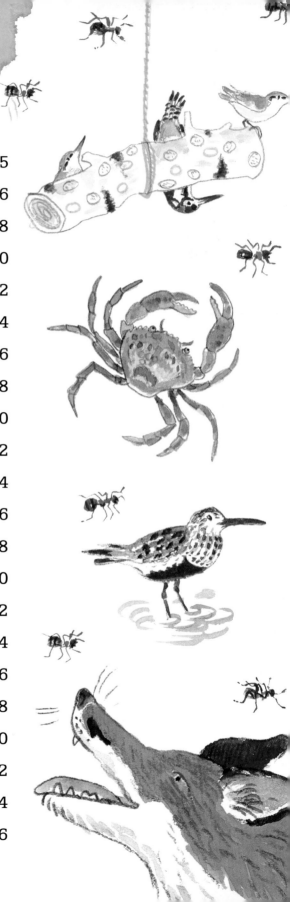

Introduction

In this book we want to share some of the ways we have fun outdoors exploring nature through play and activities with our own four children. We'll show you how to build dens and make secret signals; how to recognise star constellations and cloud shapes; how to encourage wildlife into your garden. We'll even catch you a fish, cook it on a campfire and then bake you a cake in an empty orange skin... You'll need to have grown-up help with some of the projects and you must always follow the safety guidelines, but if you follow the pages in this book, then together we can have some wild adventures!

STAY SAFE

Always follow the safety advice in the red circles. Please note that many of the traditional activities are intended to be done as a family or with adult help. So follow all the instructions very carefully, and wherever we say "with adult help" make sure a grown-up is helping you. And after all that, remember to have fun!

Woodland Adventures

Trees to climb, animals to spot, dens and hide-outs to make... There is so much going on in the woods – stop and listen to the sounds of bird calls and the creak and rustle of leaves and branches. What could be a better, ever-changing setting for wild adventures – at any time of year? There are many woodland parks and nature reserves you can explore, as well as wild woods.

The Cycle of Life

Dead and fallen trees provide food for fungi and bacteria, and these nourish a world of mini-beasts, who enrich the soil for new trees to grow. Small insects and micro-organisms also live in the leaf litter, and become food for many birds and small mammals.

Many sorts of owls love woodland, catching the small animals that live there. Owls often nest in woods too.

This is a long-eared owl.

I can feel it's a birch tree!

BAM! BAM! BAM!

Have you ever drummed on a hollow log? Woodpeckers do it – so have a go yourself and listen for a reply!

Meet a Tree

Trees are amazing, living things, and no two trees are the same; crooked or creaky, mossy or smooth, each tree has its own personality. You need at least two people for this adventure and you have to be among trees. Take turns and blindfold one person with a scarf, then take them to a tree. Without peeping, using only their senses of touch, hearing and smell, they must get to know their tree... After five minutes they are taken away a short distance and gently spun around. Take off the blindfold! Now, can they find 'their' tree?

6

Climb a Tree
Tree climbing can be fun – oak trees are great for this.

Has it got rough or smooth bark?

What sort of sound does it make?

Has it got a scent?

STAY SAFE
Never climb on rotten or mossy wood. Avoid horse-chestnut trees and willows, as their branches can easily snap.

Never climb too high or stretch too far...

Yee-hah!

and always hold on with at least one hand at all times...

In the woods, look for the signs of animal feeding activity.

Hazelnuts eaten by:

3. Vole

2. Nuthatch

1. Mouse

Beavers are common in many countries and have recently been introduced back into the UK... so if you are near water, keep your eyes open for the feeding signs left by their powerful teeth.

Squirrels leave gnawed cones lying around.

7

Games in the Woods

Secret signals, using patterns of sticks and stones, have been used for thousands of years by hunters and travelling people all over the world and, more recently, secret signs were re-invented by boy scouts and girl guides. You can have fun leaving secret signs and turn it into an exciting hide-and-seek game.

Turn left.

Go this way – over obstacles

Collect some small sticks and pebbles to carry with you, to save time.

This way.

This way.

Turn right.

Don't follow this trail.

You need to work fast!

Go this way.

'Nature chase' is a good woodland game.

8

Message this way.

Gone home/
Back to base.

Hidden! Walk 6 paces
in direction of arrow.

STAY SAFE
Don't cross
roads or deep
water.

Nature chase
Use your secret signs with this game. You'll need a family
or a gang of mates. Choose two 'lone wolves' to start as the
sign-makers and give them 20 minutes to get a good start.
The lone wolves must leave a sign about every 50 paces.
Twist and turn – don't go in a straight line – and then at
the end, HIDE! Can your wolf pack find you? A variation is
to make a trail ending in a hidden bag of sweets, and see
if the others can find it by following your trail. Maybe you
need to jot down a chart explaining each sign, in case they
forget!

They're on
our trail.

Hee-hee,
they'll never
find us here

I've found
a sign!

This way!

9

Shelters

Shelters and dens are great fun to make, and they keep you warm and dry too. If you have younger brothers and sisters, their shelter might become a sheriff's office or a bandit's hide-out. In fact your shelter can become anything you want it to be. Think up a password that you have to say before you can enter, so that only you and your mates can get in!

Make a Tent

You will need:
- Two poles about one metre/three feet high
- Tarpaulin or old sheet/blanket for a cover
- A groundsheet for inside
- Strong string or an old washing line (10 metres/30 feet)
- Wooden sticks or metal tent-pegs
- Strong string, non-plastic washing line or cord for the guy ropes

1. Hammer the two poles into the ground, about two metres/six feet apart (or find two trees about two metres/six feet apart). Stretch the string or washing line between the two sticks/trees and tie very tightly.

2. Stretch the poles taut with two long guy ropes pegged into the ground, one at each end of the tent.

3. Place your cover across the top of your string and then stretch and peg it tight with wooden sticks or metal tent pegs. To do this, you need to make some holes at the four corners of your cover, and tie on some short guy ropes, one at each corner. These keep the tent tight in the breeze. Put a plastic groundsheet inside your tent to keep out the damp when you lie inside.

1.

2.

3.

Decorate with flags or feathers

Home-made flags cut from an old shirt or skirts ↗

I could sit here all day!

Keep the sticks upright and taut with 'guy rope'

until we run out of biscuits!

10

Make a Den

You can make your den with brushwood, old sheets, tarpaulins, rope and grass – and imagination!

-ake care!

1

Don't trap your fingers!

Teepee-style

Gather branches of a similar length and tie them at the top with strong garden string. Cover with smaller branches, grass and leaves. For a waterproof finish, try an old sheet, groundsheet or tarpaulin on top.

Gloves are useful.

2.

Don't choose rotten wood.

1

Fishbone-style

If you find a tree with a fork, wedge a branch into the fork and place branches in a fishbone pattern. Cover with brushwood and straw or use your tarpaulin.

Nearly ready!

2.

Come in!

1.

I feel like Robin Hood.

Lean-to

Wedge a branch against a large boulder, but be careful the rock isn't loose and that bits are not likely to roll down on you. If you choose bendy willow branches or other bendy clippings, you can weave them together, in and out, to make a panel. Cover as before.

2. *Photograph your dens!*

Camping

Dens are fun, but camping in a real tent is something everyone should try at least once in their life! There is something magical about sleeping outdoors, 'under the stars'. A small countryside campsite with toilets and washing facilities is probably the best place to start, rather than out in the wilderness. Buy or borrow a small waterproof tent, pack a sleeping bag, a foam mat to lie on, a rucksack with some essentials – and you are ready!

Fresh water is important when you are camping.

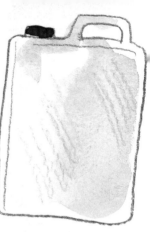

STAY SAFE
It is dangerous to drink from pools and streams. This sort of water may make you sick, so take bottled water. Always boil any drinking water you collect from nature.

String

We've chosen flat, high ground to pitch camp.

You need to stretch and peg the cords to keep the fabric tight and waterproof.

Thermos flask

Hot drinks are very important when you are outdoors for many hours.

Bucket

A portable fire bucket for barbecues is safest.

Small tarpaulin

for a quick shelter to sit on, or keep you dry in an emergency.

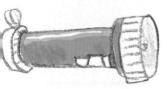

Torch ↗

Rucksack ↑

to hold all your gear

First-aid kit

Plasters, antiseptic, bandages and sting creams

Frying pan

Multi-tool ↓

Cups and plates

A pocket-knife and a small axe are very useful when outdoors, but best used by grown-ups.

Waterproof bags

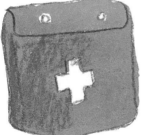

These are available from outdoor shops or online, and are very handy to keep your gear dry – especially cameras and phones.

Use Your Imagination

'Making-do' is fun when you are camping – for example, if you don't have an eggcup for your boiled egg, what do you do? Don't ask us – use your imagination! Try some scrunched-up paper towel, a sock, some moss or grass... it is all part of the fun of camping.

Evening Serenade & Dawn Chorus

Sleeping in a tent is an unforgettable experience. As darkness falls, lie back and listen to the different animals giving their evening serenade: whining mosquitoes, screeching owls, chirruping crickets, barking foxes, whistling woodcocks.... Then you fall asleep and, the next thing you know, light is filtering through the walls of the tent. It is morning, and that means it is the turn of the dawn chorus: singing birds and buzzing insects.

Divers or loons whoop and wail.

Shadow Puppets

Try making shadow puppets, using a torch, before you go to sleep!

Barn owls screech.

Screech
Screech
Screech.

It's only an owl!

What's that spooky sound?

Thrushes sing.

Mosquitoes whine.

Snipe zither and creak.

'Bzzzzz'

Woodcock whistle and grunt.

Wrens scold: Tick, tick, tick.

Crickets chirrup.

Swifts scream. eeeeeh!

Sandpiper

Bats' calls are too high-pitched to hear without a bat detector.

OOOOOOW!

Waders make sad plaintive cries.

Dunlin

Foxes scream and bark.

Campfires

The flickering flames of a campfire and the smell of woodsmoke are magical. But you need to be careful about where you light a fire, and you will need an adult with you. A safe place to try your first campfire is on a beach, where the fire can be safely put out afterwards. Some nature trails have special barbecue and campfire areas too. If you have a fire, try our suggestions for simple things to cook on it. It's an experience you never forget.

You will need:

dry wood

kindling: dry sticks, dry grass or bark.

a bucket

circle of stones ↓

How to build a fire

Make sure an adult is with you. Make a circle of stones. Clear away any surrounding twigs or dry grass that might catch alight. Put your kindling in the circle and stack some dry sticks around it in a teepee shape. Once lit, carefully feed in larger sticks until the fire is well alight. Then keep a careful eye on it and feed it every so often.

matches (keep dry in a plastic bag)

Clean up afterwards, so there is no sign of a fire.

Douse the embers with water until th are cold.

Food tastes delicious when it is cooked outdoors.

Chocolate Orange

Chocolate Oranges

1. Cut an orange in half. Eat the tasty flesh, then half-fill the orange with chocolate cake mix (use a 'just add water' packet-mix).
2. Wrap the oranges loosely in foil with their lids on (remember the cakes will rise, so leave plenty of space).
3. Place the package in the smouldering hot embers of your fire, away from direct flames.
4. After about half an hour, you'll have a cake that tastes orangey, chocolatey and a little bit smoky too. Yum!

Campfire Food

Try our campfire recipes for delicious outdoor food.

Baked Potatoes:

1. Scrub the skins clean.
2. Wrap in foil.
3. Place in the embers at the edge of the fire for about an hour, until they feel soft.
4. Eat with butter and salt. Add grated cheese if you have it.

Marshmallows:

Spear a marshmallow on a stick and hold over the fire. When crispy outside and gooey inside, it is ready to eat!

17

Canoeing Adventures

Paddle along the edge of a lake or river, and you will come close to nature. What a fantastic, peaceful experience, with the rhythmic sounds of the paddles and the trickle of water. Wildlife seems to accept humans in a canoe when it may flee from a human on two legs. Canoes are also a great way for friends, brothers and sisters, mums and dads to practise working as a team! The one at the front is the 'engine'; the one at the back paddles too, but also has to steer.

Diving ducks and grebes have beautiful markings.

Divers, also known as loons, make an eerie wailing sound.

We once got so close to a feeding beaver we heard its chomping teeth – it sounded like an old-fashioned typewriter!

Splash!

This is fun!

If a beaver is alarme it will splash its ta and dive instantly.

Rent a Canoe
Many outdoor centres rent out canoes or take groups out on canoe hikes. Perhaps there is one near where you live or where you go on holiday? Ask an adult to have a look online.

Tie reed stems together with grass. Stick a leaf on a small stick to make a sail.

Peg lilypads together with their own stalks.

Make a Mini Raft
Hold a mini–raft competition, using natural things such as lily pads, reeds, sticks, feathers and string. Award two prizes: one for the best-looking raft, and one for the raft that can float farthest.

Tie sticks together with grass, and add a paper sail.

Make a bark boat with a feather sail.

STAY SAFE
Can you swim? If not, you should learn. Always wear a life vest on the water, even if you are only going a short distance.

Look for lilypads and their long-stalked flowers – dragonflies often land on them.

19

Fishing

Make your own rod and line to catch a fish to cook for supper! It is one of those experiences in life everyone should try. Of course you might not catch a fish – but that is part of the adventure! If you don't want to kill a fish, or you aren't near a place where you could catch one – you could buy some fish instead and try our recipe with that.

Ospreys circle, hover and plunge-dive for fish.

Cormorants swim underwater to catch their fish.

Look for terns diving for fish by the sea and in large lakes.

"Be still and the earth will speak to you!"
Navajo proverb

Herons are fishing experts.

It is fun just feeding the fish!

STAY SAFE
Take great care when pulling in your line. Hooks are very sharp!

Perch taste nice but watch out for their sharp fins.

Freshly caught mackerel are a treat and can often be found for sale in seaside shops and markets.

Many lakes are stocked with rainbow trout.

Make Your Own Fishing Rod
You will need:
- A strong bendy branch such as rowan or hazel.
- Fishing line from a fishing shop
- Some fishing hooks
- Some small fishing floats or round weights.

1. Ask a grown-up to trim off any side shoots.
2. Tie your line tightly to the end – tight enough that it won't pull off when you catch a fish.
3. Thread on a small fishing float or round weight.
4. Carefully tie your hook to the line.

A small pike is tasty but it has a lot of bones.

How to Cook your Fish

You will need:
- One fish, split open, cleaned and washed by an adult.
- Tinfoil
- A small chunk of butter
- Pinch of salt

1. Wrap the fish in the foil with the butter and pinch of salt and wrap into a parcel.
2. Place it in the embers of your fire (about 15 - 20 minutes).
3. Keep checking it until the meat falls off the bones easily and is white and 'cooked'. It should smell delicious – always trust your nose!

This is a good fishing knot.

Thread like this and pull tight.

wrap your cleaned fish in foil...

...and cook it on your campfire.

Bread cheese Maggot

Bait

Animal Tracking

Muddy walks are exciting. You can splash in puddles and leave muddy footprints. And you can see animal tracks in the mud too – so keep your eyes open for their footprints and signs. It is a really good way of finding out what wildlife is living in your area. One day, on holiday in Lapland, on our way home through boggy ground, we found brown bear tracks on top of our earlier squelchy footprints.

Look on page 40 to find out how to make plaster casts so you can take animal tracks home with you.

Look at the tracks It's an animal motorway

I can't resist a frozen puddle!

Heron

Crow

Webbed feet of ducks and gulls

Beaver feeding signs

Egg eaten by a gull

Wader tracks with beak marks - a curlew.

Curlew

Beaver

Chewed feather

Chewed feather ends mean a toothed predator.

Pike eaten by an otter.

Badger

Brown bear and grey wolf.

Cat

Otter

Squirrel

Seal

shuffle marks on sand - a seal.

Stoat

Wild Boar

Fox

Mouse

Stoat and weasel

Horse wearing horseshoes

Deer

Twisted ends on a fox's dropping

Mouse droppings

Horse

Picking Berries

Elderberries often grow beside paths and in hedgerows. The leaves, stalks, twigs and unripe green elderberries are poisonous and must not be eaten. Only use the ripe blue-black berries which, when cooked, become safe to eat and make a delicious cordial when diluted with water. Blackberries (brambles) are safe to eat anytime and make delicious pies and crumbles. Get picking, but follow the safety advice!

Waxwings, sparrows and many other birds love berries

Hawks love to hunt along hedgerows for small birds.

STAY SAFE
Green elderberries are poisonous when unripe and all green parts of the plant are poisonous, so always wash your hands afterwards. Avoid roadside bushes, and pick above adult knee height to avoid berries that may have been splashed by animals' urine.

It's an elder, I recognise the smell...

...and I have checked with mum!

Elder bushes
Elder bushes have toothed pointed leaves and a sour smell. In summer the are covered with clumps of tiny white flowers. Wait for the flowers to turn into berries at the end of the summ – early September. Then pick as many of the small dark berries as you can – at least one kilo/two pounds. Elderberries are not good to eat raw, but if you cook them the are delicious. (The botanical name elder in the UK is *Sambucus Nigr* In the USA it is *Sambucus Mexic* and *Sambucus Canadensis*.)

The thick and often prickly bushes of a hedge or bramble patch are important habitats for insects, reptiles and nesting birds.

Rabbits, voles and mice live there too, attracting hungry predators such as foxes, stoats and weasels.

Blackberry and Apple Crumble

Do you have apples in your garden? If not, ask a grown-up to buy some good cooking apples – they are the perfect partner to blackberries.

You will need:
- 125g/4.5oz unsalted butter
- 75g/3.5oz caster sugar
- 200g/7oz plain flour
- 400g/14oz washed blackberries and sliced apples
- 2 heaped tablespoons extra sugar to sprinkle on the fruit

1. First wash your hands,
2. Mix the butter into the flour and sugar with your fingers until it is all mixed together like breadcrumbs. This is your crumble.
3. Gently soak the blackberries for ten minutes and then discard twigs and imperfect berries.
4. Peel the apples, and then chop them into small chunks.
5. Place all the fruit in a greased ovenproof dish, sprinkle with sugar to taste and cover with the crumble mixture.
6. With adult help, place in the oven at 170/Gas mark 4 until the fruit bubbles and topping is golden brown – about 30 minutes. Be very careful - hot fruit crumble is as dangerous as volcanic lava!

Elderberry Cordial

① Cook your berries with enough water to cover them in a large pan for 20 mins.
② Allow to cool then strain/squeeze through muslin/clean cotton tea-towel
③ For each litre (2 pints) add 1 kg (2lb) of sugar. + 12 cloves.
④ Allow to cool and store in sterilised bottles.

Mix two large spoonfuls of elderberry cordial in a mug with hot water and lemon juice.

Elder flower

Elder berries

Elderberry Cordial

STAY SAFE
Always soak all berries gently in water for a few minutes to clean them. Cook them before eating, to be safe from bugs and parasites.

Nettles and Dandelions

You can gather all sorts of food from the wild, not just berries. You know that nettles sting, but did you know they can make good soup? A walk in the woods in late spring may show you wild garlic, also known as ramsons. Use your nose; wild garlic is easily recognisable by its pungent, garlicky scent. You can make 'secret' writing using the milky sap from backyard dandelion stalks too.

Butterfly hatching

Red Admiral butterfly

Ladybird larvae eat aphids (greenfly)

Garden spider

Make Nettle Soup

Young nettle leaves can make a tasty soup when they are young and pale green, in the early summer.

You will need:
- Two handfuls of young nettle shoots
- 1 onion
- 1 potato
- A knob of butter
- A vegetable stock cube
- 1.5 litres/2 pints water

STAY SAFE
Never pick from anywhere that may have been sprayed with weedkiller or other chemicals.

Cabbage White butterfly

Butterfly caterpillar

1. Wearing gloves, pick young, pale green nettles. (Don't worry, they don't sting when they are cooked.)
3. Wash the nettles before cooking.
4. Chop the onion and the potato into small pieces.
5. Heat the butter in a saucepan.
6. Add finely chopped onion and potato. Ask a grown-up to place on a very low heat and 'sweat' for five minutes until the onion is transparent.
7. Add the washed nettle tops, water and stock cube.
8. Cover and simmer for about ten minutes (until the potato is cooked), then whiz in a blender.
9. Add salt and pepper to taste.

Nettles are an inportant home for wild life.

Wild Garlic and Cheese Mix

You will need:
- a handful of wild garlic leaves
- a handful of grated Parmesan or Cheddar cheese.
- 50gr/2oz pine nuts or walnuts
- 1 level tsp of salt
- ½ level tsp of sugar
- 100ml/3.4fl oz olive oil

Whizz it all together in a blender and keep in a jar in the fridge. Spread on toast.

STAY SAFE

Wild garlic grows in woodland, often near bluebells – be careful not to mix up the leaves when foraging. Wild garlic leaves should smell strongly of garlic.

Wild Garlic

Bluebell

Wild garlic loves shady woodland. So do woodpeckers.

Ladybird

Dandelion 'clock'

Bumblebee

Dandelion

Wild Garlic Salad

Pick a handful of wild garlic leaves in early summer. Shred them to add to your favourite salad.

Wild Garlic Toastie

Chop the garlic leaves, mix with grated cheese, spread on bread and put under the grill for a yummy veggie toasted sandwich.

Dandelion Activities

Dandelion Clocks

Have you ever blown a dandelion 'clock'? That's the fluffy seed-head of the well-known yellow flower. The seeds are spread by floating on the breeze. How many puffs to blow them all away?

Dandelion Writing

It's fun to use the sap of a dandelion for secret writing…Pick a dandelion and write with the end that is dripping milky sap. At first it is invisible – it only becomes visible later when it is dry.

I am writing something secret!

Dandelion Crown

Make a hole in the stalk with your thumbnail and thread another stalk through – keep going until you have enough to go round your head, and then join the last with the first to make a crown. You can also make necklaces or wristbands.

Sandy Shore Adventures

When you're at the seaside, at any time of year, you never know what interesting objects you'll find left behind by the tide: the bones of a sea creature, perhaps, sea-smoothed driftwood or shells, or a pile of seaweed . . . A tide-line is ever-changing and so always worth checking out. Go and explore a beach for yourself.

Gull feather

Flotsam means things that have naturally floated ashore from out at sea

Jetsam means things thrown away or washed overboard from ships or harbours.

Skulls bleached by sun and salt.

Razorbill

Otter

Gull

This must be a lobster-pot marker buoy!

Beach Sculpture
Make an eye-catching sculpture, using what you find on the beach.

Oystercatcher

Puffin

Long Jump

Beaches are great places for games such as long-jump contests. Mark out a take-off point – feet are not allowed to cross the line on the jump. Everyone chooses a stick as their own marker. Who can jump the furthest in, say, three tries each? Try different jumping techniques and different lengths of run-up.

My turn!

Jump!

Dry seaweed hair

Feather and string eyebrows

Mussel shell ears

Limpet shell eyes

Driftwood nose

Fresh seaweed beard

Look out for waders such as sanderlings. They trot along the seashore, probing the mud and sand for worms and other invertebrates.

Make a Face!
One easy game for all ages is a make-a-face competition – a collage using objects found on the tideline. Seaweed for hair and mouth, various–shaped shells for eyes and ears, feathers for eyebrows. Next time you visit the beach, make your own nature collage. Take a photo of it to keep. You can make faces in other habitats too – forest, park or garden.

29

Rocky Beach Adventures

Rocky beaches can turn up all sorts of interesting things – from pebbles and fossils to rock pools and crabs. Pebbles are amazing — every one is a unique and natural work of art. Fragments of rock are turned by time and tides into smooth shapes. Look out for seabirds too — many waders gather by the edge of the tide. Find out how to recognise the different birds and see how many you can spot.

Collect pebbles or shells with holes in and thread them toget...

Target Practice

Build a small cairn of rocks or prop up a lump of driftwood. Mark a place from which to throw and collect some nice round pebbles – make sure no one is in the way. Now, can you hit the target?

It's fun to make patterns with pebbles...

It's a question of balance!

Pebble Sculpture

Try balancing pebbles into a sculpture. Look closely, as some pebbles may contain fossils or be striped with quartz.

Cormorants hang their wings out to dry in the breeze.

Nice one!

Skimming Stones

Find some smooth flat pebbles and see how many skims you can do. You need a fairly calm sea for this. Practice makes perfect!

STAY SAFE

Never go out on rocks in stormy weather and always watch the tide – make sure you can't get cut off, or trapped against a high cliff.

Wooden handle

Line

Weight

peg

Bacon

Crabbing

Try fishing for shore crabs in rock pools. Make your own crab fishing-line from a peg, some fishing line and a bit of driftwood (see our illustration above). The crab grabs the bait and won't let go!

Keep your crabs in a bucket of water with some weed.

Always put them back where you found them afterwards!

Rockpools are amazing habitats, full of small creatures; just sit quietly and peer in. How many things can you spot?

Shore Crab

Anemone

Starfish

Hermit crab

The Pole Star
(Polaris)

The Great Bear
(Ursa Major)

The Twins
(Gemini)

The Little Bear
(Ursa Minor)

The Lion
(Leo)

The Cra
(Cancer)

Jupiter
(a planet)

If you spot
a shooting star,
make a wish!

Venus
(a planet)

32

The Hunter
(Orion)

← The Dog Star
(Sirius)

The Great Dog
(Canis Major)

Night Sky

Go outside on a clear night and look up at the stars. It's an amazing sight. Every star in every constellation is a sun, which may have planets orbiting it, just like ours. Our own sun is the nearest star to Earth, at 150 million km/ 93 million miles away. Shooting stars are bits of space debris that burn up as they hit our atmosphere, leaving a bright split-second trail. Telescopes and star-finder apps will help you - but start tonight by looking UP!

The Moon.
Watch the stages of the moon as it waxes and wanes in the night sky over about four weeks - from crescent moon to full moon and back again...

Look at the Moon
The moon is a magical sight as it moves around our planet. Waxing and waning is caused by the sun shining on its surface while the dark part is our own planet's shadow. The shapes that make 'the man in the moon' are meteor craters.

| Waxing Crescent | First Quarter | Waxing Gibbous | Full Moon |

| Waning Gibbous | Last Quarter | Waning Crescent | New Moon |

Cloud Watching

Have you noticed that different sorts of clouds often affect the weather? From fluffy cumulus to the wispy 'mares' tails' of cirrus, the 'mackerel sky' of cirrocumulus and the ominous, towering thunderclouds made by cumulonimbus. There are many sorts of clouds, and on this page we are showing you some of the commonest clouds.

Cirrus - wispy cloud formations high in the sky. Sometimes called mares' tails. 7,000m / 23,000 feet

Insects fly higher in good weather, lower in bad weather. And the swallows follow them!

Swallows have long tail-streamers and white chests.

Swifts are brown and have sickle-shaped wings.

Cumulonimbus - angry, anvil-shaped thunderclouds which can cause spectacular and scary thunderstorms!

CIRROCUMULUS – a mackerel sky; another very high cloud formation.

35

Rain, Wind and Kites

Rainy days often bring another sort of cloud – the heavy grey clouds that fill up the sky... On days like this have a go at making and decorating your own kites – and on the next windy day go and fly them! When you hold on to the string of a kite as it struggles and pulls to fly free, it feels almost like holding a living thing! Go fly a kite!

Fasten with string and tape

Kite Making

You will need: Scissors
Plastic sack
Two wooden dowels
←45cm/18inches→
←60cm/24inches→

Tape

Twine

Cut plastic to fit.

Fold over and tape

Holes

1. Place the exact middle of the cross-bar dowel about 20 cm/8 inches from one end of the spine-bar dowel. Fasten together using twine and then tape so they stay at right angles to each other in this position.

2. Tie and tape twine at one end of the cross bar, keeping it tight. Run it up to the top of the spine, make a few turns around the top tip, tie and tape – and then run it down to the other cross bar. Tie and tape. This strengthens the kite frame.

3. Lay the frame flat, with the crosspiece facing up. Cover the frame with plastic material such as a bin bag. Use tape to fix it to the frame and cut it to fit.

4. Make two small holes in the plastic along the spine (see diagram) and strengthen these holes with tape. Feed a length of twine about 20 cm/8 inches long through the hole at the top and tie it to the spine. Do the same with the other end of the twine at the other hole. This is your 'bridle'.

7. Attach the rest of your ball of twine to the bridle. This is your kite-string. By choosing where you attach the string, you control the angle at which the kite flies. You might need to try it out to find the best spot, but start near the top of the bridle.

8. Attach a length of twine, about 100 cm/3 feet long, to the bottom end of the spine as a tail. Tie cloth or plastic streamers to it at regular intervals.

Bows, Catapults and Whistles

These can be great fun to make and very exciting to use. The whistle is a good test of your skill so have fun – but be careful and always do these activities with grown-up help. You can practise your target skills and making skills too. Take great care, and always follow the Stay Safe tips. When you make your whistle, a twisting motion helps the bark slide off in one piece.

You need adult he for thi

Remember to bend the bow into a curve as you tie on the string.

You need to find a supple, bendy stick.

Cut grooves in each end to hold the string.

STAY SAFE

Make sure an adult is with you when you use bows and catapults. Never point bows or catapults at each other or at animals. Always put a cork on your arrow and always stand behind whoever is firing a bow or catapult.

Make a Bow

1. Cut a bendy branch about one metre/three feet long.
2. Make a shallow notch at each end of the branch to hold your bow-string.
3. Tie the string to the first notch.
4. Bend the bow before tying garden twine to the second notch, so that the bow is curved. When you fire your bow stand sideways on to your target and keep your firing arm straight. If you enjoy it, there may be a local archery club you can join and learn to fire a real bow and arrow safely.

Make an Arrow

Choose a straight stick about 60 cm/2 feet long. Cut a triangle of card from a cereal box and fold in half. Carefully split one end of your arrow and insert the card. Put tape round this end of the arrow to stop the split end relaxing. Put a wine cork on the tip of the arrow. Make more!

Hold the arrow betwee your fingers like this.

Make a Catapult

Find a stick with a natural 'Y' shape and trim it to size. Make some shallow grooves to hold the elastic. You'll need about 20 cm/8 inches of strong elastic (or rubber bands knotted or looped together) knotted to either side of the ammo holder, attached to your patch of leather or strong cloth in the middle. Make a target from an old milk carton or plastic bottle. Hold the ammo between your fingers, tucked in the cloth... aim and fire!

Grooves cut in each fork

Forked stick

Acorns are good ammo.

Leather or cloth patch

Rubber bands looped together or elastic string.

A Rowan Whistle

Rowan or willow is the best wood as the bark comes away easily.

← 15 cm/6 inches →

1) Cut a branch as thick as a finger...

2) Cut the mouthpiece at an angle

3) Make this cut. →

Clean it up with a cut at the end.

4) Cut all the way round the bark.

5) With another stick or branch, tap around the whistle end until the bark is loose enough to ease off!

⑤

You will need this later...

⑥ Make the 'V' shape deeper and cut a slice off here

This is where you will blow.

⑦ Slide the bark sheath back on.

⑧ Blow and listen. You've made your own whistle!

39

Skulls, Pellets and Plaster Casts

Skulls, pellets and tracks left in mud or sand are such exciting finds you may wish you could bring them home. Well, why not? Some schools have nature tables displaying nature finds that children and teachers bring in to share – that's a great idea. Here are some different ways to bring home and display your finds in a collection.

Sheep skull

Make a Plaster Cast

Buy some Plaster of Paris powder from a pharmacy. It is the same stuff that's used for broken arms and legs and it sets very hard, very quickly. Carry it in a plastic bag in a rucksack to keep it dry and mix it on the spot. Follow the instructions on this page. The plaster gets warm as it dries and will take about 20 minutes to set. It's a good idea to wear gloves.

How to Make a Plaster Cast

You will need:
- Rucksack
- Gloves
- Plaster of Paris
- A waterproof bag to keep the Plaster of Paris in
- A strip of card held in shape with paper clips
- A bottle of water
- A mixing jug

Put your gloves on. Tip the Plaster of Paris into the jug. Mix it with the water, using a stick, until it is about the consistency of thick yoghurt. Use your strip of cardboard held by paper clips to adjust the size of the mould to fit the track. A set of two or four tracks will need a bigger mould; perhaps you can adapt a cardboard box? Experiment!
Pour in the mixture about 5 cm/2 inches deep. The bigger the mould, the deeper the plaster needs to be.

Water

Mixing jug

Cardboard strip

Clip ↗

Fox tracks

40

...ry sun-bleached
skulls may just need a
shake and a brush down
with an old toothbrush.

Always wear gloves.

Rinse the skull in clean
water. Ask an adult to
help you.

Goose skull

Clean a Skull

If you are lucky, you may find a skull or some bones when you're exploring outdoors – on a beach, for example. Sometimes these bones are old enough to have been cleaned and sun-bleached by nature, so that they will just need a quick clean when you get home. If you are unlucky, bones and skulls can have flesh still attached, or even maggots; if so, then these skulls are best looked at, photographed and left where they lie! But try going back at a later date to check if they are 'ready'.

STAY SAFE
Always wear gloves and wash your hands after you've been handling or cleaning items for your collection.

Pellets

Fur

Vole skulls

...og skull

Bones

Shrew jaws

Ribs

Jaw

Teeth

Bird skull

Feather

Shrew skull

Owl Pellets

Owl pellets are not poo! They are packages of dry bones, neatly wrapped in fur and feathers and regurgitated through the beak. Look for owl pellets under trees or old barns, where owls like to roost or nest; or under fence posts where they might perch at night. But if you don't find any, don't worry – you can now buy owl pellets online from school suppliers. Many birds cough up pellets but owl pellets are the ones that contain the most bones, teeth and skulls. Soak a pellet in warm water for a few minutes to soften it and then tease it apart with forceps. Glue the bones onto a card, using PVA glue.

41

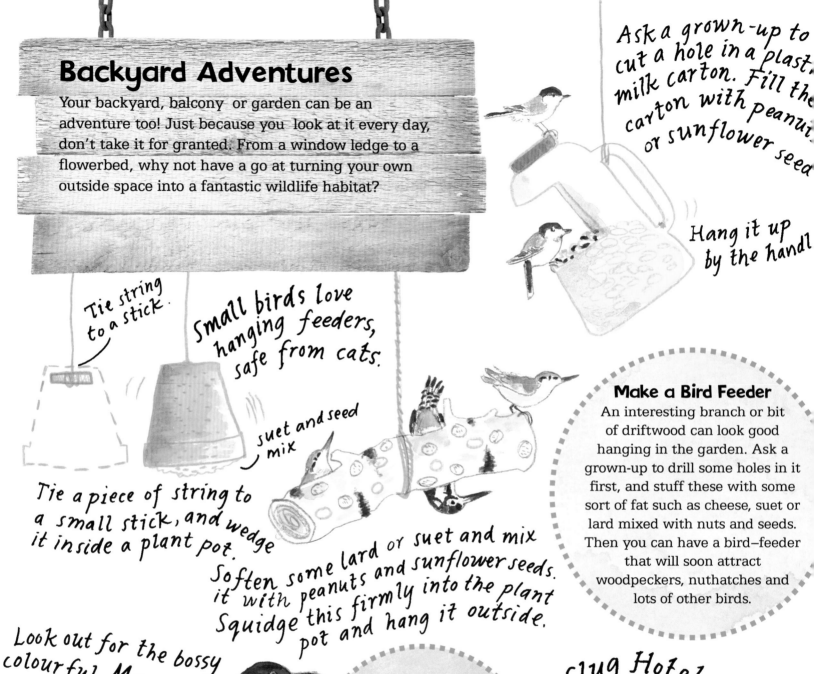

Backyard Adventures

Your backyard, balcony or garden can be an adventure too! Just because you look at it every day, don't take it for granted. From a window ledge to a flowerbed, why not have a go at turning your own outside space into a fantastic wildlife habitat?

Ask a grown-up to cut a hole in a plast. milk carton. Fill the carton with peanut or sunflower seed

Hang it up by the handl.

Tie string to a stick.

Small birds love hanging feeders, safe from cats.

suet and seed mix

Tie a piece of string to a small stick, and wedge it inside a plant pot.

Soften some lard or suet and mix it with peanuts and sunflower seeds. Squidge this firmly into the plant pot and hang it outside.

Make a Bird Feeder

An interesting branch or bit of driftwood can look good hanging in the garden. Ask a grown-up to drill some holes in it first, and stuff these with some sort of fat such as cheese, suet or lard mixed with nuts and seeds. Then you can have a bird–feeder that will soon attract woodpeckers, nuthatches and lots of other birds.

Look out for the bossy colourful Magpie.

Make a Slug Hotel

Take half a melon or a hollowed-out grapefruit. Cut a door in the side, and put it on the ground. Lift it up from time to time, to keep a note of what creatures shelter inside.

Slug Hotel

Bug B & B

Hollow bamboo sticks or garden cuttings, bound together, make a good shelter for insects such as bees and lacewings.

An old watering can wedged in a sheltered spot makes a good nesting place.

Make a Bird Table

A bird table provides food for birds all year round. You can make one from a wooden tray. Ask an adult to help you screw or nail it to a post or windowsill. You could have several at different heights.

Put Up a Nesting Box

A nesting box can be bought from garden centres or online, Set it up in a sheltered spot and see if a bird chooses to nest in it!

Hammer and nails

Hooks and eyes

Wooden tray

Wooden Post

Our birds will love this!

You can also fix your table to a wall or windowsill.

43

Try to identify your finds in books and on nature websites.

Pussy Willow

Catkins

Horse-chestnut bud

Find pretty buds in the spring.

Fishing p. 20-21

Take snaps!

Make a shell face p.29

Making a boat p.19

Butterfly wing

Jetsam p. 28

Fox fur found on a fence

Thread pebbles with holes. p. 30

Make a plaster cast. p. 40

Keep a sketch book

Pot

44

Nature Tables and Collections

A nature display is a great way to bring all your fantastic wild experiences home with you: feathers, shells, berries, leaves, plaster casts, beachcombing treasures. Make or buy some labels to write the dates you found your objects, as well as the name and location, then display them in vases, airtight jam jars, zip-lock plastic bags. When not on display, store them in empty boxes at home. What wonderful ways to remember your Wild Adventures.

Black Elk of the Sioux Nation once said: 'May you always walk in beauty!'

Wow - let's go!

Collect lovely seed heads and berries in the autumn.

Make a nice display on your windowsill or on a small table.

Autumn leaves have lovely colours.

driftwood

aning a
ull p.41

sea urchin

pecked egg shell

Pinecone to tell the weather p.35

Conker

Fossils

mooth coloured glass

Owl pellet p.41

Acorn

Beech mast

Crabbing p.31

bbit droppings

Sycamore seeds

Find feathers and decorate your shelter. p.10

Glossary

Bacteria – micro-organisms that help with decay – other sorts cause many diseases.

Bait – food used to entice and catch a fish or other animal.

Bat detector – a machine that helps us listen to the high-pitched calls of bats.

Collage – a picture made by sticking different things, such as paper or fabric, onto a backing.

Constellation – a cluster of stars that makes a pattern which looks like an object or figure.

Cordial – a sort of fruit drink.

Dawn Chorus – the early morning song of birds.

Dowel – a man-made stick of wood, usually round in cross-section.

Driftwood – wood washed ashore.

Fungi – organisms like mushrooms and toadstools.

Gibbous – Stage of the moon when the illuminated part is greater than half but less than a full moon.

Guy ropes – ropes that hold a tent taut and stop it collapsing.

Invertebrates – insects without backbones such as worms.

Kindling – small, dry bits of wood used to get a fire started.

Larva (plural larvae) – the first stage of an insect's life after it has hatched. A caterpillar for example.

Micro-organisms – tiny life forms that can only be seen under a microscope.

Muslin – a loosely woven cotton cloth.

Planet – planets move round (orbit) stars. Earth is a planet which orbits the Sun.

Plaster of Paris – a white powder that sets like rock when mixed with water.

Predator – an animals that preys on others for food.

Sterilise – to clean so well there are no germs or bacteria, in boiling water for example.

Teepee – a cone-shaped tent built around wooden poles.

Waders – birds with long legs that feed on wetlands and seashores.

Wilderness – unfarmed and often uninhabited landscapes such as forests and mountains.